MIXED MARTIAL ARTS

MMA: FEROCIOUS FIGHTING STYLES

Frazer Andrew Krohn

Abdo & Daughters
MIDDLE GRADE NONFICTION

An imprint of Abdo Publishing
abdobooks.com

ABDOBOOKS.COM

Published by Abdo Publishing, a division of ABDO, PO Box 398166, Minneapolis, Minnesota 55439.
Copyright © 2023 by Abdo Consulting Group, Inc. International copyrights reserved in all countries.
No part of this book may be reproduced in any form without written permission from the publisher.
Abdo & Daughters™ is a trademark and logo of Abdo Publishing.

102022
012023

THIS BOOK CONTAINS
RECYCLED MATERIALS

Design: Kelly Doudna, Mighty Media, Inc.
Production: Mighty Media, Inc.
Editor: Liz Salzmann
Cover Photograph: Gregory Payan/AP Images
Interior Photographs: A.RICARDO/Shutterstock Images, pp. 11, 24, 50–51, 54, 55 (top), 60 (bottom left), 61 (top left); Ahturner/Shutterstock Images, p. 40; Andre Luiz Moreira/Shutterstock Images, pp. 46, 56–57; Andy Brownbill/AP Images, pp. 26, 61 (bottom right); Camerasandcoffee/Shutterstock Images, p. 12 (bottom); Cassiano Correia/Shutterstock Images, pp. 12 (top), 27, 32, 33, 55 (bottom); Celso Pupo/Shutterstock Images, p. 21; Corey Sipkin/AP Images, p. 59; Dawid S Swierczek/Shutterstock Images, pp. 18 (top), 25, 52; ECKEHARD SCHULZ/AP Images, p. 13; Everett Collection Inc/Alamy Photo, p. 37; Featureflash Photo Agency/Shutterstock Images, p. 44; gaikova/Shutterstock Images, pp. 38–39; Isaac Brekken/AP Images, pp. 4–5, 6, 61 (top right); John Locher/AP Images, pp. 7 (left), 42; Jose Juarez/AP Images, p. 58; joyfull/Shutterstock Images, p. 18 (bottom); Kathy Hutchins/Shutterstock Images, p. 49; Krabikus/Shutterstock Images, p. 47 (top); Kris Krug/Wikimedia Commons, p. 48; Leo Correa/AP Images, p. 35; lev radin/Shutterstock Images, p. 17; Llyn Hunter/Wikimedia Commons, pp. 53 (top), 60 (top right); Marco Crupi/Shutterstock Images, p. 30; mark reinstein/Shutterstock Images, p. 16; maRRitch/Shutterstock Images, p. 47 (bottom); MartialArtsNomad/Wikimedia Commons, pp. 28–29; MikhailSk/Shutterstock Images, pp. 8–9; Miljan Zivkovic/Shutterstock Images, pp. 10, 60 (bottom right); Photo Works/Shutterstock Images, p. 20; R. Lemieszek/Shutterstock Images, pp. 14–15; Raoul Gatchalian/STAR MAX/IPx/AP Images, p. 7 (right); Ryan Remiorz/AP Images, p. 45; Stefan Holm/Shutterstock Images, p. 41; swissmacky/Shutterstock Images, pp. 22–23, 60 (top left); UfaBizPhoto/Shutterstock Images, p. 19; Victor Joly/Shutterstock Images, pp. 53 (bottom), 61 (bottom left)
Design Elements: Mighty Media, Inc.; mkirarslan/iStockphoto; sanchesnet1/iStockphoto

Library of Congress Control Number: 2022940769

Publisher's Cataloging-in-Publication Data
Names: Krohn, Frazer Andrew, author.
Title: MMA: ferocious fighting styles / by Frazer Andrew Krohn
Description: Minneapolis, Minnesota : Abdo Publishing, 2023 | Series: Mixed martial arts | Includes online resources and index.
Identifiers: ISBN 9781532199219 (lib. bdg.) | ISBN 9781098274412 (ebook)
Subjects: LCSH: MMA (Mixed martial arts)--Juvenile literature. | Mixed martial arts--Juvenile literature. | Hand-to-hand fighting--Juvenile literature. | Ultimate fighting--Juvenile literature. | Sports--History--Juvenile literature.
Classification: DDC 796.81--dc23

CONTENTS

The Money Fight 5

Mixed Martial Artists 9

Boxing 15

Kickboxing and Muay Thai 23

Brazilian Jiu-Jitsu 29

Wrestling 39

Other Fighting Styles 51

Future Fighting Styles 57

Timeline 60

Glossary 62

Online Resources 63

Index 64

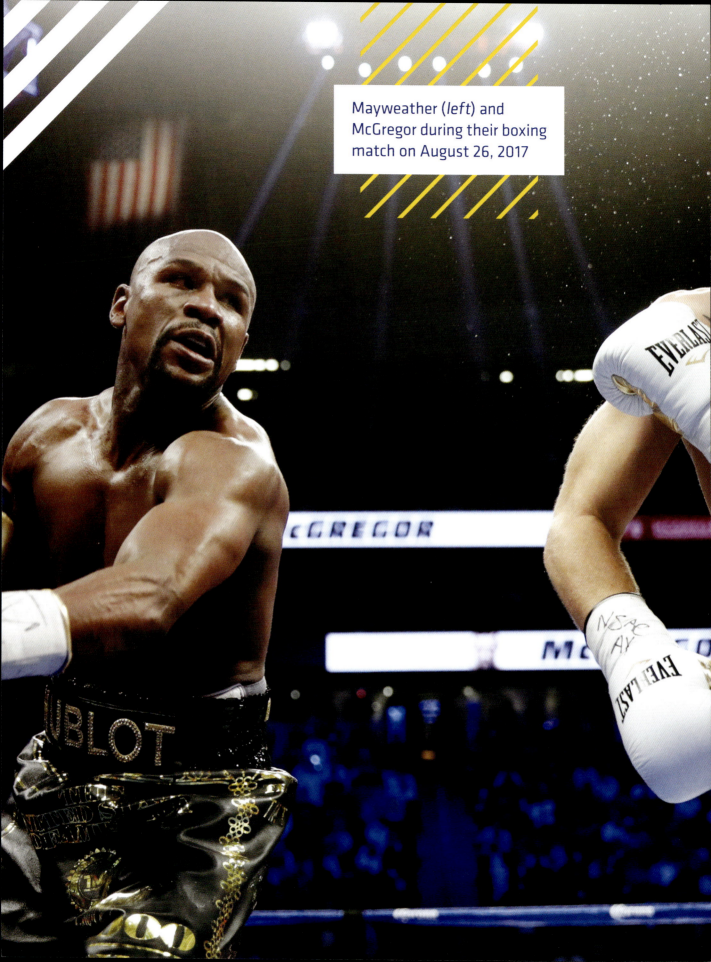

Mayweather (*left*) and McGregor during their boxing match on August 26, 2017

CHAPTER 1

THE MONEY FIGHT

Conor McGregor of Ireland is a top mixed martial arts (MMA) fighter with a record of 22 wins and 6 losses. He was the first Ultimate Fighting Championship (UFC) fighter to hold UFC championships in two weight classes at the same time. McGregor primarily uses a boxing fighting style, relying on powerful strikes to knock out opponents.

Because of his interest in boxing, McGregor proposed a boxing match between himself and legendary American boxer Floyd Mayweather Jr. Mayweather was a 15-time world champion boxer with a record of 49-0. Mayweather agreed, and the match was scheduled for August 26, 2017. Due to the star power of both fighters, the event was expected to make a huge amount of money for everyone involved. Therefore, it made sense for the fight to be called the Money Fight.

Although McGregor came from a boxing background, he had never fought a professional boxing match. However, most of his MMA wins were on knockouts. So, many thought that McGregor's power and size could possibly cause problems for Mayweather. But in the end, it was a boxing match, not an MMA fight, and McGregor was in the ring with one of the best boxers of all time.

McGregor started strong, winning the first few rounds. But he began to tire quickly. Mayweather had expected this and did his best to avoid McGregor's punches in the early rounds. Then, as McGregor continued to tire, Mayweather went on offense and was able to overwhelm the Irishman. Mayweather knocked McGregor out in the 10th round.

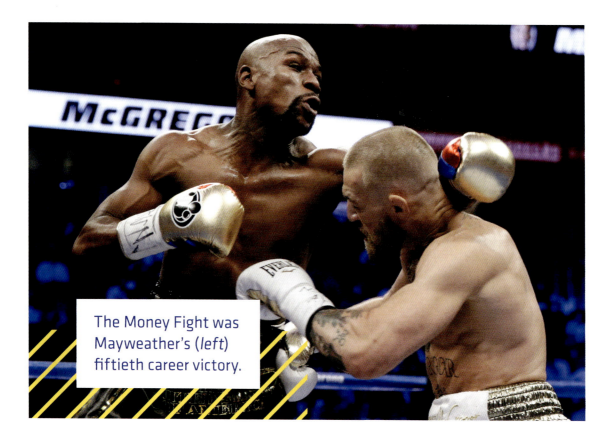

The Money Fight was Mayweather's (*left*) fiftieth career victory.

MMA ALL-STAR
CONOR McGREGOR

Conor McGregor was born July 14, 1988, in Dublin, Ireland. When he was 12, he joined a boxing club. In 2006, he started training in MMA and won 12 of his first 14 professional fights. McGregor joined the UFC in 2013, becoming the UFC featherweight champion in 2015. The next year, he won the UFC lightweight championship. This made him the first to hold titles in two divisions. McGregor's behavior and trash talk outside the Octagon earned him the nickname Notorious. He is an exciting fighter who draws thousands of fans.

McGregor (*left*) beat José Aldo (*right*) to win his first UFC championship.

Many UFC fighters began training in martial arts when they were children.

CHAPTER 2

MIXED MARTIAL ARTISTS

Being a mixed martial artist means using many different fighting techniques together. It is far more straightforward to learn and perfect one technique. Learning multiple techniques and using them together effectively is far more difficult. This is why so few find success in the UFC, Bellator, or other high-level MMA promotion.

A fighter who trains in just one fighting style will likely struggle as they try to advance in MMA. Being one-dimensional can only get a fighter so far. In regional competition, a fighter can get away with using fewer styles, but if they make it to the national and world stages, their weaknesses will be exposed.

Brazilian fighter Edson Barboza is an example of a fighter who struggled as soon as he made it to the world championship level. Starting in 2009,

Learning Brazilian jiu-jitsu helps MMA fighters learn defensive skills.

he fought with the Renaissance and Ring of Combat promotions, gaining a record of seven wins and no losses. The next year, he joined the UFC.

Barboza made his UFC debut on November 20, 2010, against Mike Lullo. At the time, Barboza was known for his striking skills. He defeated Lullo with leg kicks, becoming the first person in UFC history to finish a fight that way.

There are hundreds of UFC fights every year.

ULTIMATE FIGHTING CHAMPIONSHIP

The Ultimate Fighting Championship is, without a doubt, the premier MMA promotion in the world. Founded in 1993, the UFC would become the first mainstream MMA promotion. Those in the UFC had to deal with the setbacks, aid in rule progression, and be accountable for any early missteps. As the popularity of MMA grew, the UFC created more weight classes in order to make fights safer, fairer, and more competitive. Today, it's widely accepted that UFC champions are the best MMA fighters in the world.

Before becoming a mixed martial artist, Barboza was a kickboxer.

Khabib Nurmagomedov

In spite of being a fearsome striker, Barboza lacked the wrestling skills to compete consistently against the elite UFC fighters. He could be dominated on the ground by fighters such as Russian Khabib Nurmagomedov. This showed Barboza's inability to deal with fighters skilled in wrestling. There was clearly a hole in Barboza's game.

DIFFERENT FIGHTING STYLES

There are many different martial arts that can be utilized during an MMA fight. At the first UFC event in 1993, each of eight competitors represented a different fighting style. These were savate, sumo, kickboxing, American Kenpo, Brazilian jiu-jitsu (BJJ), boxing, shootfighting, and taekwondo.

The least effective of these styles was arguably sumo, represented by Teila Tuli. Tuli fought savate fighter Gerard Gordeau in the first UFC fight. Gordeau knocked Tuli out in just 26 seconds. Since then, there has only been one other sumo wrestler in the UFC. This was Yarbrough, who competed at UFC 3. Although he did better than Tuli, he still lost in under two minutes.

It soon became clear that a fighter cannot be one-dimensional and make it in the highest levels of MMA. This is often addressed during training. A good coach will not let their students neglect any areas of the MMA game. Today, the four most common styles MMA fighters train in are boxing, kickboxing, BJJ, and wrestling.

Yarbrough (*left*) began competing in sumo in 1992. At his heaviest, he was 704 pounds (319 kg)!

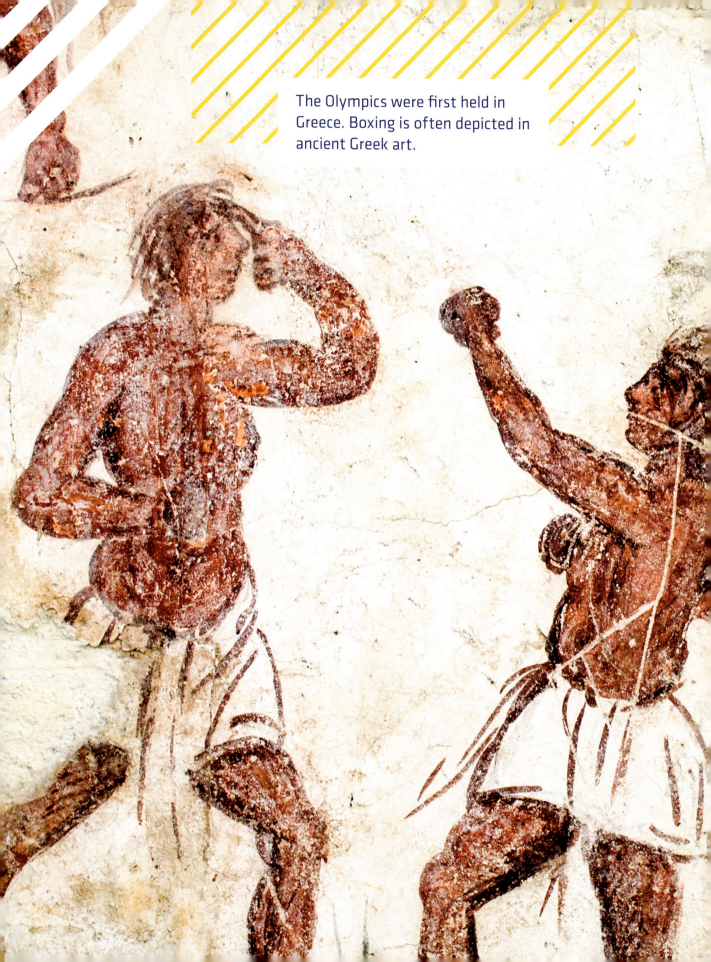

The Olympics were first held in Greece. Boxing is often depicted in ancient Greek art.

CHAPTER 3

BOXING

Since ancient times, humans have battled one another as a way to settle disputes, often by using their fists. Boxing first appeared as an Olympic event in 688 BCE. The official rules of boxing followed today were established in 1867. These are known as the Marquess of Queensberry Rules.

Many high-level MMA fighters started out in boxing, having been inspired by famous boxers in history. Some of the most famous boxers of all time include Muhammad Ali, Mike Tyson, Rocky Marciano, Sugar Ray Leonard, and Joe Louis.

BOXING IN MMA

The importance of boxing within MMA is obvious. Like in boxing, MMA fights start with the two competitors standing facing each other. This means that an MMA fighter has to be confident fighting in this position.

Boxing for MMA differs from pure boxing in a number of ways. Boxing focuses on throwing and avoiding punches. There isn't much emphasis on clinching. And there is no kicking, kneeing, elbowing, or takedowns allowed in boxing. Doing any of these can lead to points being taken away or even a disqualification. In MMA, all of these techniques are legal and are used in the vast majority of MMA fights.

Another difference is the gloves worn by the fighters. Boxing gloves are big, padded gloves that force the hand into a fist shape. The gloves protect the fighter's hands when punching. Boxers wrap

Ali was known for his speed and quick footwork.

In boxing, fighters are not allowed to hit opponents below the belt or in the back of the head or neck.

their hands with layers of tape before putting on the boxing gloves. The wrapping further protects their hands.

Boxing gloves vary in size and weight depending on the weight class. The bigger the gloves, the more protection a boxer gets. Boxers can block shots with their gloves, allowing for better defense. There is also less risk of injury from getting hit by an opponent wearing boxing gloves.

MMA gloves are thin and the same for all fighters, regardless of weight class. The gloves are fingerless, allowing for more precision when grappling. However, the gloves' thinness doesn't allow for much wrapping underneath, often leading to hand injuries.

MMA gloves have less padding, so they don't prevent cuts and bruises as well as boxing gloves.

Blows from boxing gloves are cushioned and cause less physical damage than blows from MMA gloves.

TRAINING

There is no denying that training in boxing for an MMA fight is vital. Every fight starts on the feet, so boxing skills are important. Sparring and hitting punching bags and speedbags are boxing training techniques that MMA fighters also commonly use.

MMA fighters spar in two different ways. Sometimes they spar using full MMA rules, mixing in takedowns and grappling. But MMA fighters will also spar according to boxing rules in order to improve footwork, technique, timing, and speed.

Professional MMA fighters may spar several times a week to prepare for a fight.

CROSSOVERS

Although MMA fighters commonly train in boxing techniques, it can be challenging for fighters to switch from one to the other. As McGregor's attempt to cross over from MMA to boxing in the Money Fight showed, it doesn't always turn out well. And going the other way isn't any easier.

In January 2010, boxer James Toney discussed fighting an MMA match with UFC president Dana White. At that time, Toney was a well-respected boxer with an impressive 44 knockouts. He had held world titles in three different weight classes. Toney and White came to a deal. Toney faced former UFC heavyweight and light heavyweight champion Randy Couture in August 2010. Couture was known for his solid overall MMA game but most notably his wrestling.

What played out in this fight demonstrated what can happen if a fighter doesn't have a well-rounded MMA game. Couture took Toney down within 15 seconds, and Toney never got back to his feet. Couture used multiple dominant positions before submitting Toney with ease. It proved that a fighter must be skilled in all facets of MMA, not just one.

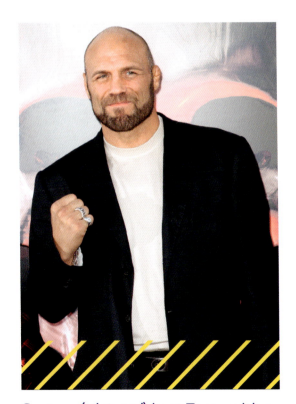

Couture (*pictured*) beat Toney with a triangle choke.

Aldo (*right*) returned to soccer during a 2014 charity match in Brazil.

MMA FIGHTERS OUTSIDE MMA

Often, MMA fighters will participate in specific martial arts events in order to increase their skills in those disciplines. These commonly include BJJ and wrestling tournaments. And, some notable athletes have switched from other sports to MMA. For example, UFC featherweight champion Alexander Volkanovski competed in rugby before switching to MMA. And, former featherweight champion José Aldo was first a promising soccer player. And finally, Greg Hardy fought 13 MMA matches after playing several seasons in the National Football League.

Muay Thai is also known as Thai boxing. It is the national sport of Thailand.

CHAPTER 4

KICKBOXING AND MUAY THAI

Kickboxing is a relatively new martial art, having originated in the 1960s. It is heavily influenced by Muay Thai, which started in Thailand in the 1200s. Muay Thai is known as the art of eight limbs because it uses fists, elbows, knees, and shins. Muay Thai fighters and kickboxers fight in a four-sided ring surrounded by ropes, the same as in boxing.

It is important for MMA fighters to learn the kicking side of MMA. Since MMA fights start on the feet, kicking can be a vital technique in a fighter's success. Kicks can serve several purposes in an MMA fight. Obviously, they're used to hurt an opponent in order to try and win a fight. But they can also be used to push an opponent away or set up a takedown. Kicking usually delivers a much more powerful strike than punching, as a fighter uses more of their body to produce force. Even if a kick is blocked, the power often shocks opponents, giving the kicker an advantage.

Kicking does come with risks, however. The fighter has to momentarily stand on one leg to kick, so they could be knocked off-balance more easily. Another risk is having a kick checked. This is when a fighter realizes their opponent is about to kick their legs and turns their shin or knee toward the kicker's leg to block the kick. A famous example of this is when Anderson Silva and Chris Weidman squared off for the UFC middleweight title on December 28, 2013. In the second round, Weidman checked

Silva (*right*) is considered one of the best MMA fighters of all time. He left the UFC in 2020.

Silva's leg kick attempt. Silva's leg broke on the impact. The referee stopped the fight and Weidman won the match on a TKO.

In spite of the risks, there are still many advantages to kicking. Some of the most famous knockouts in MMA history have come via head kicks. During the January 2012 fight between Edson Barboza and Terry Etim, Barboza spun in a circle and connected his heal with Etim's temple. It knocked Etim out instantly. This move won Barboza the Knockout of the Year in 2012.

Similarly, during a June 2019 flyweight championship fight, Valentina Shevchenko landed a vicious head kick on Jessica Eye, knocking her out. The power that a fighter can produce when throwing a head kick often means that if it lands, it's lights out for their opponent.

Eye was unconscious for several minutes following Shevchenko's head kick.

One of the most effective kickboxers to transition from pure kickboxing to MMA is the UFC middleweight champion Israel Adesanya. Adesanya began kickboxing in 2010 and quickly progressed to the premier kickboxing promotion, Glory. He transitioned to MMA in 2012 and entered the UFC in 2018.

Adesanya achieved a phenomenal 20-0 record, dominating opponents with his stand-up game. His kickboxing background made him very skilled at distance management. This made him able to land kicks on his opponent and not get hit with a countershot. Adesanya's kickboxing skills greatly helped his MMA career. In April 2019, he became middleweight champion.

Israel Adesanya in 2019

LEG KICKING EVOLUTION

The leg kick in MMA has evolved over time. The first fighter to use a calf kick in a major MMA fight was former UFC lightweight champion Benson Henderson in 2011. Henderson used them to strike his opponents' lower legs and set up further attacks.

Traditionally, fighters attacked the legs using kicks focusing on the inside and outside of the thigh. Although this can be effective, there has been an evolution in recent years. The calf kick has become an important element in many fighters' games. The reason for this is that the calf is far more vulnerable than the thigh. The calf has less muscle and also has many nerves that can affect balance and strength if targeted.

There have been multiple fights in which a fighter's foot appeared to stop working because the nerves were compromised by calf kicks. Going forward, we can expect to see more fighters incorporating the calf kick into their MMA game to become even more dangerous during fights.

A calf kick helped fighter Rafael Dos Anjos (*pictured*) defeat Neil Magny in 2017.

Former MMA fighter Royce Gracie (*right*) is a BJJ instructor. He is Helio Gracie's son.

CHAPTER 5

BRAZILIAN JIU-JITSU

The history of BJJ dates back to the early 1900s. Jiu-jitsu is an ancient Japanese fighting style. In the 1800s, Jigorō Kanō founded a form of jiu-jitsu called judo. Mitsuyo Maeda learned judo from Kanō, becoming a groundwork expert. He left Japan in 1904 to demonstrate his skills to the world. He traveled to many different countries, arriving in Brazil in 1914.

Brazilian fighter Carlos Gracie attended a judo presentation put on by Maeda. Instantly hooked, Gracie became Maeda's student. Gracie would go on to teach his younger brother, Helio, the knowledge he had gained from Maeda. The Gracies then developed BJJ. This fighting style focuses on dominating opponents on the ground, using an opponent's power against them and ultimately trying to force them into a submission.

A rear-naked choke cuts off blood to the brain. This can render an opponent unconscious.

The effectiveness of BJJ really came to light at UFC 1. Royce Gracie entered the tournament as a BJJ fighter. Gracie wore the traditional BJJ *gi* and was a far smaller competitor than some of his opponents. He ended up winning the championship, submitting all of his opponents on the way to the final. Gracie was extremely impressive, as was BJJ.

In the final match of UFC 1, Gracie submitted Gerard Gordeau, who was much heavier. Gordeau weighed 216 pounds (98 kg), whereas Gracie was just 176 pounds (80 kg). Despite this, Gracie was able to get the fight to the ground and finish Gordeau in under two minutes with a rear-naked choke. This is when the attacker positions themself behind their opponent and squeezes their neck with their forearms. This is one of the most common submissions in MMA.

JIU-JITSU IN TODAY'S MMA

After the success of BJJ at UFC 1, it quickly rose in popularity. BJJ continues today to be one of the most effective martial arts fighting styles used by top MMA fighters. A number of BJJ fighters have become world champions. UFC champion Charles Oliveira holds the record for the most submissions in UFC history, with 15 opponents tapping out because of his BJJ skills. UFC Hall of Famer and former lightweight and welterweight champion B.J. Penn also proved just how effective BJJ can be in MMA, having captured both belts via submission.

Demian Maia and Ronaldo Souza were two Brazilian competitors who mainly used BJJ to dominate opponents. Their style clearly worked, as both men got to the top of the sport. Souza recorded 14 submissions during a career that saw him capture the Strikeforce middleweight title. Maia has twice competed for UFC championships, coming up short on both occasions. Nevertheless, he has recorded 14 submissions during his career. Maia is one of the most famous BJJ competitors in the UFC.

In September 2018, Oliveira (*left*) beat Christos Giagos (*right*) for his eleventh submission win.

There are some risks with being purely a BJJ competitor, however. BJJ can be overwhelmingly effective if a fighter can get the fight to the ground. But if they can't, BJJ competitors may find themselves in trouble. If a fighter's main game plan is to get their opponent to the ground and submit them, they may struggle if their opponent has a solid defense. When Demian Maia came up short in

In 2020, Maia (*pictured*) opened a BJJ academy and museum in São Paulo, Brazil.

both of his championship fights in 2010 and 2017, it was because he failed to get the fight to the ground. He was not able to work his BJJ game. His failures during these fights highlighted how limiting BJJ can be.

Similarly, in 2018, world-renowned BJJ competitor Mackenzie Dern entered the UFC with a phenomenal grappling record. She has two World Jiu-Jitsu Championship gold medals and one gold medal from the ADCC Submission Wrestling World Championship. ADCC is the premier grappling competition for jiu-jitsu competitors. Dern has also won gold at the 2016 BJJ World Cup. She had fought on the regional scene, starting her career with a 5-0 record before joining the UFC.

However, after joining the UFC, weaknesses in her overall MMA game became apparent. There's no denying that she is possibly the best BJJ competitor in women's MMA. She sometimes struggles to get opponents down to the ground, so she has to rely on her stand-up game. But her stand-up abilities, as well as her wrestling, often let her down. Her abilities in these areas are behind that of other competitors in her division.

UNUSUAL SUBMISSIONS IN MMA HISTORY

Although chokes and armlocks are common in MMA today, fighters sometimes use unusual submissions. These include the twister, the Ezekiel Choke, and the inverted triangle. These are difficult moves that aren't used very often. But when a fighter uses one successfully,

Dern began training in BJJ when she was three years old.

FIGHTIN' WORDS

Here are some common terms used in MMA.

FIGHT CARD // a program or list of the matches during an MMA event. The card usually has one or two headline, or main, matches plus several warm-up, or preliminary, matches.

GRAPPLE // to fight using holds and wrestling moves rather than punches or kicks.

KNOCKOUT (KO) // when one fighter has been knocked down and is unable to get up and resume fighting within a specified time.

ROUND // one of the periods of time a fight is divided into. MMA fights have three or five five-minute rounds with a one-minute rest between each round.

STRIKE // a blow delivered to an opponent while standing. A strike can be made by a fist, knee, elbow, or foot.

SUBMISSION // when a fighter wins by grabbing their opponent in a painful hold that they can't break free of, so that they are forced to give up.

TAKEDOWN // a move that forces or knocks an opponent to the ground.

TAP OUT // when a fighter taps the mat with their hand to indicate that they want to give up.

TECHNICAL KNOCKOUT (TKO) // when a fight referee stops a match because one of the fighters is too injured to continue.

the fight usually has a memorable ending.

The twister is a choke hold that involves a sideways body bend and neck crank. It affects the spine and neck, which is why it's so effective. It is also extremely difficult to pull off, so there have only been two successful ones in UFC history. Chan Sung Jung did it against Leonard Garcia in 2011, and Bryce Mitchell did it against Matt Sayles in 2019.

The Ezekiel Choke is another uncommon submission. It consists of pressing the opponent's throat with one hand while using the other hand to create pressure. In order to pull it off, the opponent has to be on top. It's extremely difficult, which is why Alexey Oleynik is the only fighter to pull it off in UFC competition. He did it twice in UFC competition and 12 times in total.

The inverted triangle is where the attacker tries to isolate their opponent's arm and shoulder by wrapping it with their legs in a triangle shape. This leads to reduced blood flow to the brain, which often leads to submission. In 2009, Imada won Submission of the Year by using an inverted triangle choke on Jorge Masvidal. Imada got into a position where he was upside down on Masvidal's back while Masvidal was still standing. Imada was able to squeeze enough to cause Masvidal to go unconscious. It's considered one of the wildest submissions in MMA history.

Imada won Submission of the Year at the 2009 World MMA Awards.

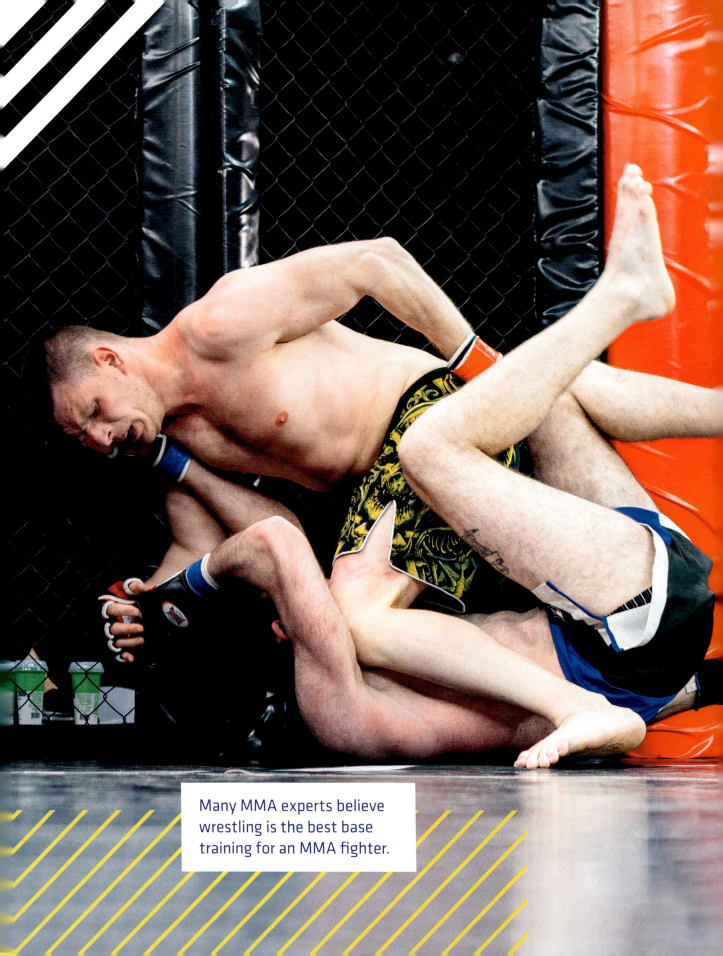

Many MMA experts believe wrestling is the best base training for an MMA fighter.

CHAPTER 6

WRESTLING

Wrestling is the most dominant fighting style in MMA today. No fighter can make it to the top without a solid wrestling game. Wrestling, in some form, has been around since 3000 BCE, making it one of the oldest competitive sports in the world. It has also been an Olympic sport since 708 BCE. If a fighter doesn't have a strong wrestling background, they still can make it to the main stage of the UFC or Bellator. However, when they compete against the best fighters in the world, they often come up short.

Training in wrestling usually begins in high school or college. Wrestling involves using the entire body to pin an opponent. Many believe that having strong wrestling skills helps a fighter control where a fight goes. The fighter can either keep the fight standing using a takedown defense or move the fight to the ground by using a takedown.

MMA fighter Ed Ruth (*in blue*) was a wrestler at Penn State University.

WRESTLING TECHNIQUES

A fighter with a wrestling background usually wants to take the fight to the ground, where they will have an advantage. There are several ways for a fighter to take their opponent down. These include single- or double-leg takedowns and trips. The goal of any of these takedown techniques is to end up on top of the opponent.

A single-leg takedown is when the attacker grabs one of their opponent's legs and tries to knock them off-balance. In a double-leg takedown, the attacker steps toward their opponent and wraps their arms around the opponent's hips or legs. They

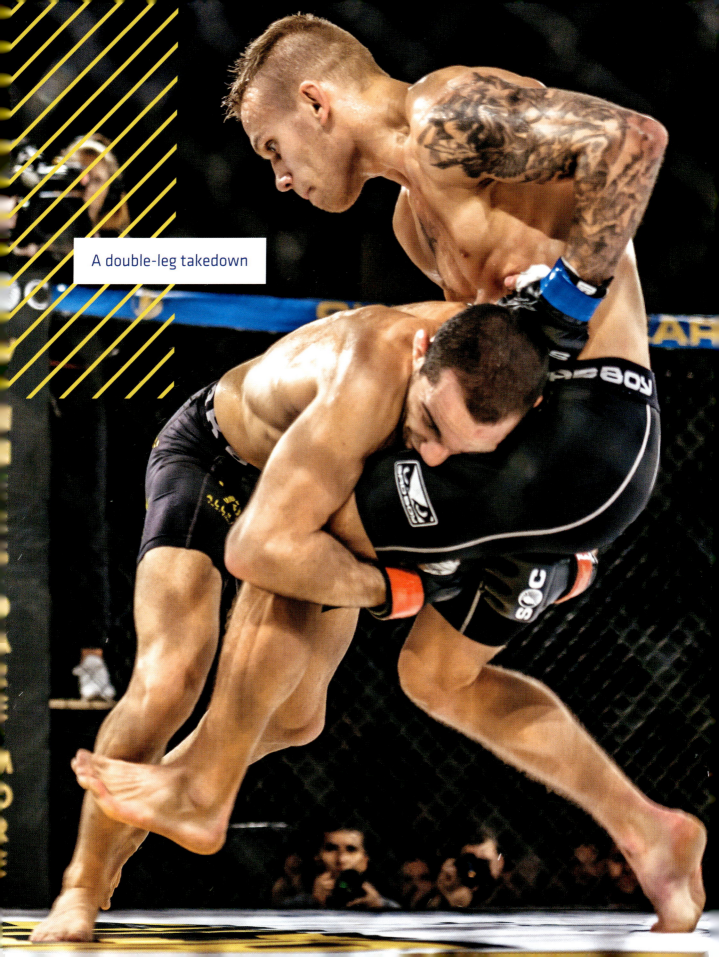

A double-leg takedown

then drive forward to complete the takedown while the opponent is unable to free their legs and regain balance.

Trips are effective as they usually allow a fighter to get their opponent to the floor without having to defend a countermove. A trip starts when the fighters are close to each other or grappling. Then one fighter pushes the other backward while wrapping a leg around one of the opponent's legs. This can be achieved by wrapping the leg either inside or outside the opponent's leg. Takedowns and trips use an opponent's weight to catch them off-balance.

Nurmagomedov takes down McGregor.

One way for a fighter to defend against a takedown attempt is to hold their hands lower and prepare to block a low move. But this position can open them up to being hit with a big shot to the head. For example, when McGregor faced Nurmagomedov in October 2018, Nurmagomedov had made a successful takedown in the first round, so McGregor expected another takedown attempt in the second round. McGregor left his hands low to defend against it. Instead, Nurmagomedov dipped his head slightly, as if he were going for a takedown, before landing a huge overhand right punch to McGregor's jaw, knocking him down.

GEORGES ST-PIERRE

Known as one of the best wrestlers in UFC history, Georges St-Pierre is a phenomenon in the MMA world. Despite having no wrestling experience before starting MMA, St-Pierre has recorded 90 takedowns, the most in the UFC. St-Pierre says his background in karate has contributed to his success in picking up wrestling so well. Many karate techniques are designed to bring an attacker closer to their opponent, which is needed for an effective takedown.

One of St-Pierre's best fights was when he faced Josh Koscheck in August 2007. Koscheck is a four-time Division I National Collegiate Athletic Association (NCAA) All-American and NCAA wrestling champion. This means that Koscheck has strong wrestling skills. But that night, St-Pierre dominated Koscheck using his wrestling fighting style. St-Pierre landed multiple takedowns, was able to control Koscheck on the ground, and defended against any takedown attempts from Koscheck.

St-Pierre also recorded victories over Jon Fitch, Thiago Alves, Nick Diaz, Dan Hardy, and Carlos Condit. His takedown record in these fights was 44–0, meaning he took his opponents down 44 times and he wasn't taken down once. The most impressive of these was against Fitch, who is a world-renowned wrestler. This proves just how dominant St-Pierre was in the wrestling realm of MMA and how dominant wrestling can be overall. St-Pierre retired in 2019 and entered the UFC Hall of Fame in 2020.

Georges St-Pierre

IS WRESTLING BORING?

Despite being such an important element in MMA, many view wrestling as boring compared to striking. Sometimes, even when a wrestler dominates their opponent, they don't actually do much damage. They take their opponent down and land just enough strikes and positional changes to keep the referee from making them stand up and start over. This happens when the referee determines that a fighter is stalling in a position. The referee has the fighters stand up and start again to encourage a more entertaining fight.

St-Pierre (*left*) won a rematch against Koscheck (*right*) at UFC 124 in 2010.

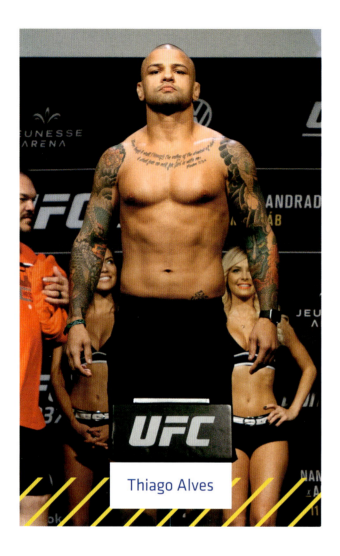

Thiago Alves

If a fighter takes their opponent down early in the fight, the crowd can get bored, especially if the fighters aren't doing much damage to each other. It can be difficult for fans in the audience to see grappling exchanges, so they have to rely on the big screens in the arena to see what's going on, rather than watching the ring directly. In these situations, the crowd may boo the fighters involved, again highlighting that wrestling can come across as boring. Further, some people believe that wrestling isn't a "real" fight. They feel that lying on an opponent to attempt a submission without causing much injury is just trying to win on the judges' scorecards.

Like St-Pierre, some of the most dominant MMA fighters in history have succeeded through wrestling. Nurmagomedov is widely considered one of the greatest wrestlers of all time. He has a background in sambo, a Russian style of grappling. Nurmagomedov's fighting style was to wrestle his opponents, dominate them, and overwhelm them with positional control.

Some MMA fans have called for the UFC to make a rule against stalling.

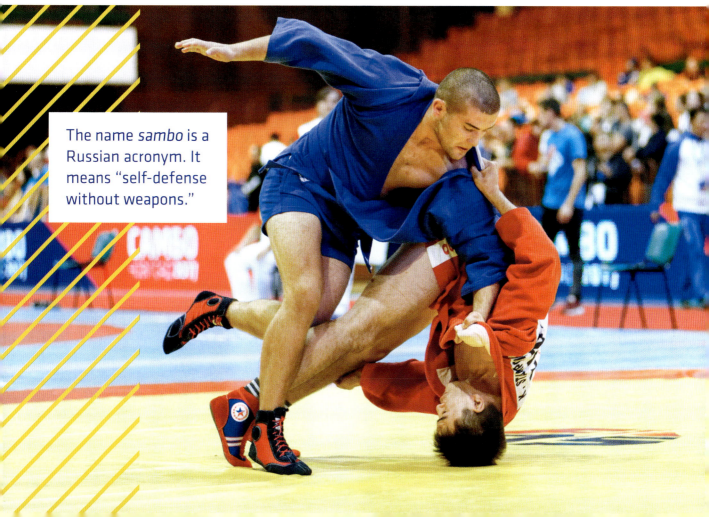

The name *sambo* is a Russian acronym. It means "self-defense without weapons."

Another prominent wrestler is UFC welterweight champion Kamaru Usman. He has dominated every opponent he has faced in the UFC. Usman relies mainly on a wrestling-heavy approach. He has a background in high school wrestling, which arguably gave him the skills he required to dominate in MMA.

Other successful wrestlers include Bellator welterweight champion Yaroslav Amosov and Bellator heavyweight champion Ryan Bader. Amosov is a four-time sambo world champion and holds a record of 26-0. He dominated the majority of his opponents through grappling. Bader also prefers to take his opponents down and use a grappling-heavy approach to win fights.

Many find a back-and-forth exchange of punches and kicks more entertaining than watching one fighter lying on the other for an entire fight. However, wrestling is a legal fighting style allowed inside the Octagon, and it has proven to be very effective. Fighters who are dominated by wrestlers need to improve their takedown defense and overall grappling skills.

Ryan Bader

CM Punk in 2011

THE PUNK EXPERIMENT

In 2014, former World Wrestling Entertainment (WWE) champion CM Punk signed with the UFC. He was one of the biggest stars that the WWE had ever produced. UFC president Dana White hoped that his popularity would cross over to MMA fans. CM Punk's first UFC bout was against Mickey Gall in September 2016. Despite the massive hype around him, CM Punk failed to land a single significant strike. Gall choked him out in about two minutes. But CM Punk didn't give up. He returned to face Mike Jackson in June 2018. Jackson also dominated him, winning in a unanimous decision. So, the UFC's experiment with CM Punk didn't work. It seems that professional wrestling isn't the best style to transition to MMA!

MMA fighter Rose Namajunas (*right*) trained in taekwondo as a child. She is known for her head kicks.

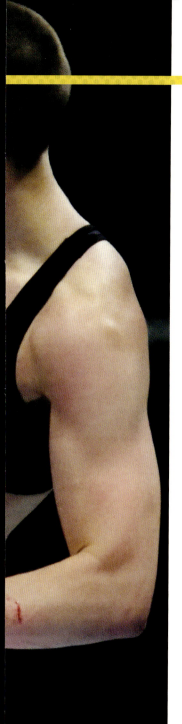

CHAPTER 7

OTHER FIGHTING STYLES

While boxing, kickboxing, BJJ, and wrestling are the main styles used in MMA, they aren't the only ones seen in the MMA Octagon. Other martial arts styles have also worked well. These include taekwondo, judo, and karate.

TAEKWONDO

Former UFC lightweight champion Anthony Pettis and his brother, Bellator bantamweight champion Sergio Pettis, are both taekwondo fighters. Taekwondo is a Korean martial art. *Tae* means "to break with the foot," *kwon* means "to break with the fist," and *do* means "the art." Taekwondo focuses on punching and kicking techniques. Taekwondo translates well into MMA because it encourages fighters to be on their toes, landing strikes on their opponents and avoiding getting hit themselves.

This style has led to great success for the Pettis brothers. An excellent example of the effectiveness of taekwondo occurred when Anthony Pettis faced Benson Henderson in December 2010 at the final World Extreme Cagefighting event. Pettis used his taekwondo skills to run at and spring off of the cage fence, landing a flying roundhouse kick on Henderson's chin. This is considered one of the greatest strikes in MMA history.

UFC women's flyweight champion Shevchenko started learning taekwondo at age five before switching to Muay Thai and kickboxing.

JUDO

Like wrestling and jiu-jitsu, judo is a grappling martial art with a long and interesting history. Created in 1882 by Jigorō Kanō, judo became an Olympic sport in 1964. Judo's principles are to lift and throw your opponent onto their back. When on the ground, submissions are used to either choke the opponent or lock a joint until they tap out.

Judo throws have to be adapted for use in MMA. In traditional judo, competitors wear the *gi*. A fighter can grab their opponent's *gi* to conduct the throws and submission holds. But MMA fighters don't wear *gi*, so they have to learn to use headlocks and armlocks to grip their opponents. Although it isn't easy, it can be extremely effective.

Ronda Rousey is a pioneer of women's MMA and one of the biggest names the UFC has ever seen. Rousey earned a bronze medal in judo at the 2008 Olympic Games. Then she transitioned successfully into MMA with a judo fighting style. Rousey began her MMA career with 12 straight finishes, including nine submissions that used her judo background.

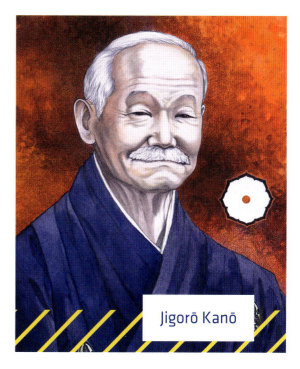

Jigorō Kanō

Judo fighters wearing *gi*

Possibly the greatest example of Rousey using her judo background is when she threw Alexis Davis during their title fight in July 2014. Rousey used a head and arm throw. Then she followed up with punches to knock Davis out in just 16 seconds. Rousey put judo on the MMA map. However, it is a much less common fighting style in today's MMA.

KARATE

Karate is a Japanese martial art that dates back to the 1600s. The fighting style uses punches and kicks as well as strikes with the knees, elbows, and open hand. In karate, fighters stand partly sideways to each other. This provides less of a target

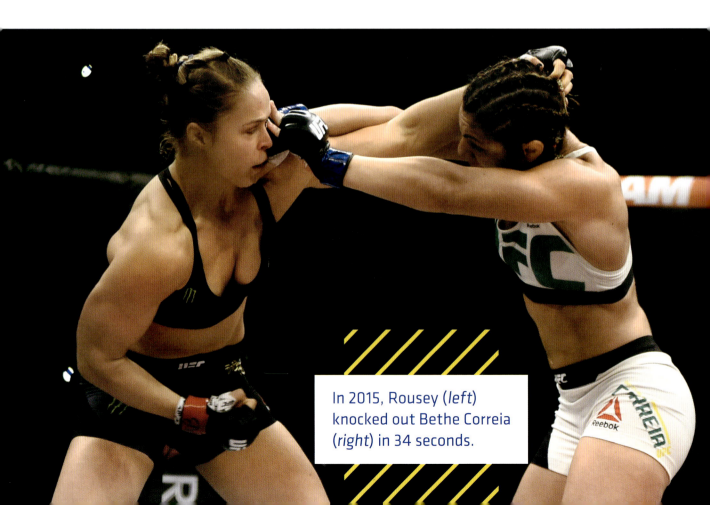

In 2015, Rousey (*left*) knocked out Bethe Correia (*right*) in 34 seconds.

for an opponent than if fighters faced each other straight on. Karate fighters also concentrate on their footwork. They aim to move quickly to get close to their opponents to attack and to also get out of danger.

There have only been a handful of world-class karate practitioners that have made it to the highest level of MMA. One reason for this is that becoming skilled in karate requires more practice than most other martial arts. It is a difficult style to pick up as part of MMA training. Top UFC fighters with backgrounds in karate include Stephen Thompson, Michael Page, Georges St-Pierre, and Machida. They have each either held a UFC title or competed in a title fight in a major MMA organization.

Making quick, powerful strikes is an important element of karate.

Machida won the UFC light heavyweight championship in 2009.

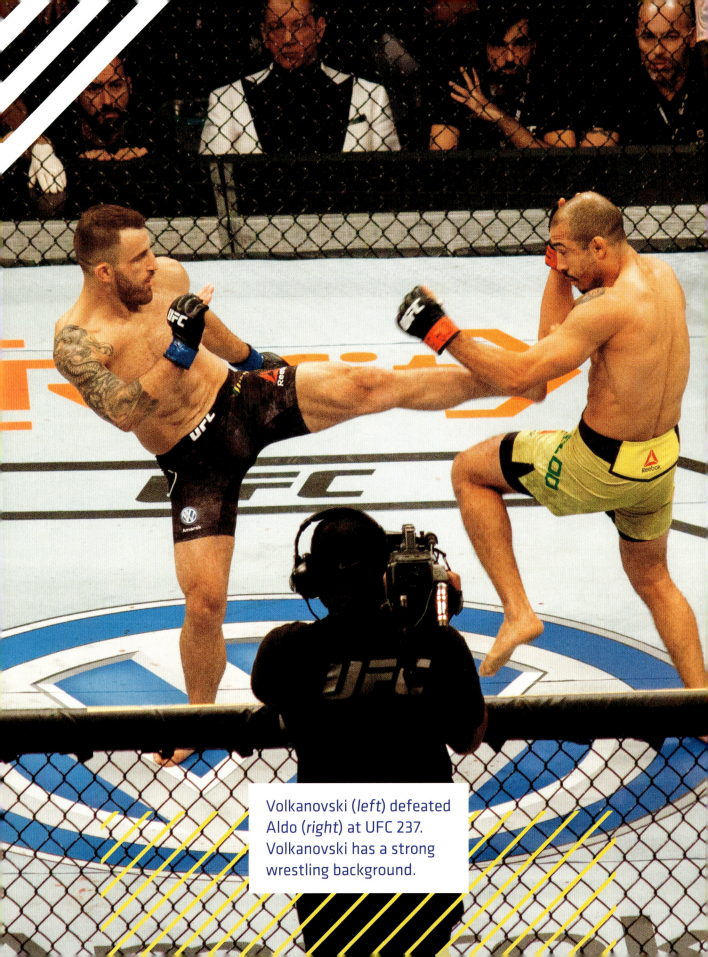

Volkanovski (*left*) defeated Aldo (*right*) at UFC 237. Volkanovski has a strong wrestling background.

CHAPTER 8

FUTURE FIGHTING STYLES

Wrestling continues to evolve and will remain a dominant element of MMA. It has become clear that wrestling is the most solid base for entering MMA, so this trend will likely continue. The fact that there have been more UFC champions from wrestling backgrounds than any other fighting style speaks for itself.

Additionally, some fighters today start MMA training without first specializing in a specific style. This trend is also likely to continue, with more fighters entering the premier promotions skilled in techniques from different martial arts. A fighter who enters the Octagon with just one fighting style will likely be exposed as one-dimensional and will not succeed at the highest level.

In December 2017, Ngannou (*left*) knocked Alistair Overeem (*right*) out in the first round.

But we shouldn't be surprised to see occasional exceptions, such as Francis Ngannou. He defeated Stipe Miocic in March 2021 to become the UFC heavyweight champion. Ngannou is known for his powerful strikes. He has little wrestling experience, so he is a fairly one-dimensional fighter. But his punches are so strong that if he can remain on his feet, he usually wins with his heavy knockout power.

As MMA grows in popularity, exciting new fighters will showcase their styles as they compete to be the best. Major promotions such as the UFC, Bellator, and ONE Championship will continue to produce competitive fights with a wide array of different fighting styles. The mix of styles means fans can look forward to many exciting fights!

In December 2021, Usman (*right*) became the UFC's overall best fighter. He started out as a wrestler.

MMA ENDGAME

An MMA fight ends with either a finish or a judges' decision. A finish is when one fighter wins before the end of the rounds. This includes winning by submission, knockout, technical knockout, or disqualification. If neither fighter finishes by the end of the last round, then the winner is determined by the three fight judges. If all three judges choose the same winner, it's called a unanimous decision. If they don't all agree, it's called a split or majority decision. The winner is the fighter chosen by two of the judges.

TIMELINE

Wrestling becomes
an Olympic event.
708 BCE

Muay Thai is
developed in
Thailand.
1200s

Jigorō Kanō
creates judo.
1882

Kickboxing
starts being
developed.
1960s

688 BCE
Boxing becomes
an Olympic event.

1600s
Karate is
developed
in Japan.

EARLY 1900s
Brazilian jiu-jitsu
is developed.

The Ultimate Fighting Championship is formed, and UFC 1 is held.
1993

Edson Barboza knocks out Terry Etim with a head kick, winning 2012 Knockout of the Year.
JANUARY 2012

The Money Fight between McGregor and Mayweather Jr. takes place.
AUGUST 2017

1964
Judo becomes an Olympic sport.

2011
Benson Henderson is the first fighter to use a calf kick in an MMA fight.

APRIL 2019
Israel Adesanya becomes UFC middleweight champion.

GLOSSARY

All-American—chosen as a member of an honorary college team featuring the best athletes in their sport.

arguably—supported by reasons or evidence.

armlock—a hold that forces an opponent's arm to bend backward at the elbow or shoulder.

clinching—a wresting move in which a fighter grabs their opponent while they are standing up.

debut—a first appearance.

disqualification—barred from competition or from winning a prize or a contest.

footwork—the skill with which the feet are moved.

gi—the traditional robe worn by people who practice martial arts such as judo and karate.

hype—promotional publicity designed to create excitement about something.

incorporate—to include or work into.

mainstream—the ideas, attitudes, activities, or trends that are regarded as normal or dominant in society.

NCAA—National Collegiate Athletic Association. The NCAA supports student athletes on and off the field. It creates the rules for fair and safe play.

one-dimensional—having one main style or technique, rather than a combination of many styles and techniques.

practitioner—one who practices a certain profession, sport, or craft.

premier—first in rank, position, or importance.

promotion—an organization or company that organizes MMA fights and tournaments.

showcase—to exhibit something to try to get others to like it.

technique—a method or style in which something is done.

unconscious—asleep, knocked out, or otherwise unaware of what's going on.

vulnerable—able to be hurt or attacked.

ONLINE RESOURCES

To learn more about MMA fighting styles, please visit **abdobooklinks.com** or scan this QR code. These links are routinely monitored and updated to provide the most current information available.

INDEX

ADCC Submission Wrestling World Championships, 34
Adesanya, Israel, 26
Aldo, José, 21
Ali, Muhammad, 15
Alves, Thiago, 44
American Kenpo, 13
Amosov, Yaroslav, 48

Bader, Ryan, 48
Barboza, Edson, 9–10, 12, 25
Bellator, 9, 39, 48, 51, 59
BJJ World Cup, 34
boxing, 5–7, 13, 15–17, 19–20, 23, 51
Brazil, 9, 29, 31
Brazilian jiu-jitsu (BJJ), 13, 21, 29–32, 34, 51

Condit, Carlos, 44
Couture, Randy, 20

Davis, Alexis, 54
Dern, Mackenzie, 34
Diaz, Nick, 44

Etim, Terry, 25
Eye, Jessica, 25
Ezekiel Choke, 34, 36

Fitch, Jon, 44

Gall, Mickey, 49
Garcia, Leonard, 36
Glory, 26
Gordeau, Gerard, 13, 31
Gracie, Carlos, 29
Gracie, Helio, 29
Gracie, Royce, 30–31

Hardy, Dan, 44
Hardy, Greg, 21
Henderson, Benson, 27, 52

Imada, Toby, 37
injury, 17, 25, 46
Ireland, 5–7

Jackson, Mike, 49
Japan, 29, 54
jiu-jitsu, 29, 34, 52
judo, 29, 51–54
Jung, Chan Sung, 36

Kanō, Jigorō, 29, 52
karate, 43, 51, 54–55
kickboxing, 13, 23–27, 51
Knockout of the Year, 25
Korea, 51
Koscheck, Josh, 43

Leonard, Sugar Ray, 15
Louis, Joe, 15
Lullo, Mike, 10

Machida, Lyoto, 55
Maeda, Mitsuyo, 29
Maia, Demian, 31–32, 34
Marciano, Rocky, 15
Marquess of Queensberry Rules, 15
Masvidal, Jorge, 37
Mayweather, Floyd, Jr., 5–6
McGregor, Conor, 5–7, 20, 43
Miocic, Stipe, 58
Mitchell, Bryce, 36
Money Fight, 5, 20
Muay Thai, 23

National Collegiate Athletic Association (NCAA), 43
Ngannou, Francis, 58
Nurmagomedov, Khabib, 12, 43, 46

Octagon, 7, 48, 51, 57
Oleynik, Alexey, 36–37
Oliveira, Charles, 31
Olympic Games, 15, 39, 52–53
ONE Championship, 59

Page, Michael, 55
Penn, B.J., 31
Pettis, Anthony, 51–52
Pettis, Sergio, 51–52
Punk, CM, 49

Renaissance, 10
Ring of Combat, 10
Rousey, Ronda, 53–54
Russia, 12, 46

sambo, 46, 48
savate, 13
Sayles, Matt, 36
Shevchenko, Valentina, 25
shootfighting, 13
Silva, Anderson, 24–25
Souza, Ronaldo, 31
St-Pierre, Georges, 43–44, 46, 55
Strikeforce, 31
Submission of the Year, 37
sumo wrestling, 13

taekwondo, 13, 51–52
Thailand, 23
Thompson, Stephen, 55
Toney, James, 20
training, 9, 13, 19–20, 39
Tuli, Teila, 13
Tyson, Mike, 15

UFC Hall of Fame, 31, 44
Ultimate Fighting Championship (UFC), 5, 7, 9–13, 20, 24, 26–27, 30–31, 34, 36–37, 39, 43, 48–49, 51, 53, 55, 57–59
United States, 5
Usman, Kamaru, 48

Volkanovski, Alexander, 21

Weidman, Chris, 24–25
weight classes, 5, 7, 11, 17, 20–21, 24–27, 31, 48, 51, 58
White, Dana, 20, 49
World Extreme Cagefighting, 52
World Wrestling Entertainment (WWE), 49
wrestling, 12–13, 20–21, 34, 39–40, 42–44, 46, 48, 51–52, 57–58

Yarbrough, Emmanuel, 13